For my mother, who taught me to care about the world's children.
P. M.
For my sister Geia, everyone's sweetheart.
Love, L. L.

2% of the publisher's proceeds will be donated to
Heifer International
1015 Louisiana Street
Little Rock, AR 72202
http://www.heifer.org
This nonprofit organization is working to end global hunger while caring for the earth by providing livestock and training to people in need. Heifer creates sustainable small-scale farm enterprises which help people lift themselves out of poverty. All recipients agree to "pass on the gift" of their animals' first offspring to others in need, building stronger communities and, ultimately, a better world.

First Aladdin Paperbacks edition July 2004

Text copyright © 2001 by Page McBrier
Illustrations copyright © 2001 by Lori Lohstoeter

ALADDIN PAPERBACKS
An imprint of Simon & Schuster
Children's Publishing Division
1230 Avenue of the Americas
New York, NY 10020

Also available in an Atheneum Books for Young Readers hardcover edition.
Designed by Ann Bobco
The text of this book was set in Cantoria.

Manufactured in China
30 29 28 27 26 25 24 23

The Library of Congress has cataloged the hardcover edition as follows:
McBrier, Page.
Beatrice's goat / by Page McBrier; illustrated by Lori Lohstoeter.-1st ed.
p. cm.
"An Anne Schwartz book"
Summary: A young girl's dream of attending school in her small Ugandan village is fulfilled after her family is given an income-producing goat. Based on a true story about the work of the Heifer project.
ISBN 978-0-689-82460-9 (hc.)
1. Heifer Project—Juvenile fiction. [1. Heifer Project—Fiction. 2. Goats—Fiction. 3. Blacks—Uganda—Fiction. 4. Uganda—Fiction.] I. Lohstoeter, Lori, ill. II. Title.
PZ7.M4783Be 2000 [E]—DC21 99-27018
0115 SCP
ISBN 978-0-689-86990-7 (pbk.)

Beatrice's Goat

BY PAGE MCBRIER

ILLUSTRATED BY LORI LOHSTOETER

Aladdin Paperbacks

New York London Toronto Sydney

If you were to visit the small African village of Kisinga in the rolling hills of western Uganda, and if you were to take a left at the crossroads and follow a narrow dirt path between two tall banana groves, you would come to the home of a girl named Beatrice.

Beatrice lives here with her mother and five younger brothers and sisters in a sturdy mud house with a fine steel roof. The house is new. So is the shiny blue wooden furniture inside. In fact, many things are new to Beatrice and her family lately.

And it's all because of a goat named Mugisa.

Beatrice loves everything about Mugisa . . . the feel of her coarse brown-and-white coat, the way her chin hairs curl just so, and how Mugisa gently teases her by butting her knobby horns against Beatrice's hand—*tup, tup*—like a drumbeat waiting for a song.

But there is one reason why Beatrice loves Mugisa most of all.

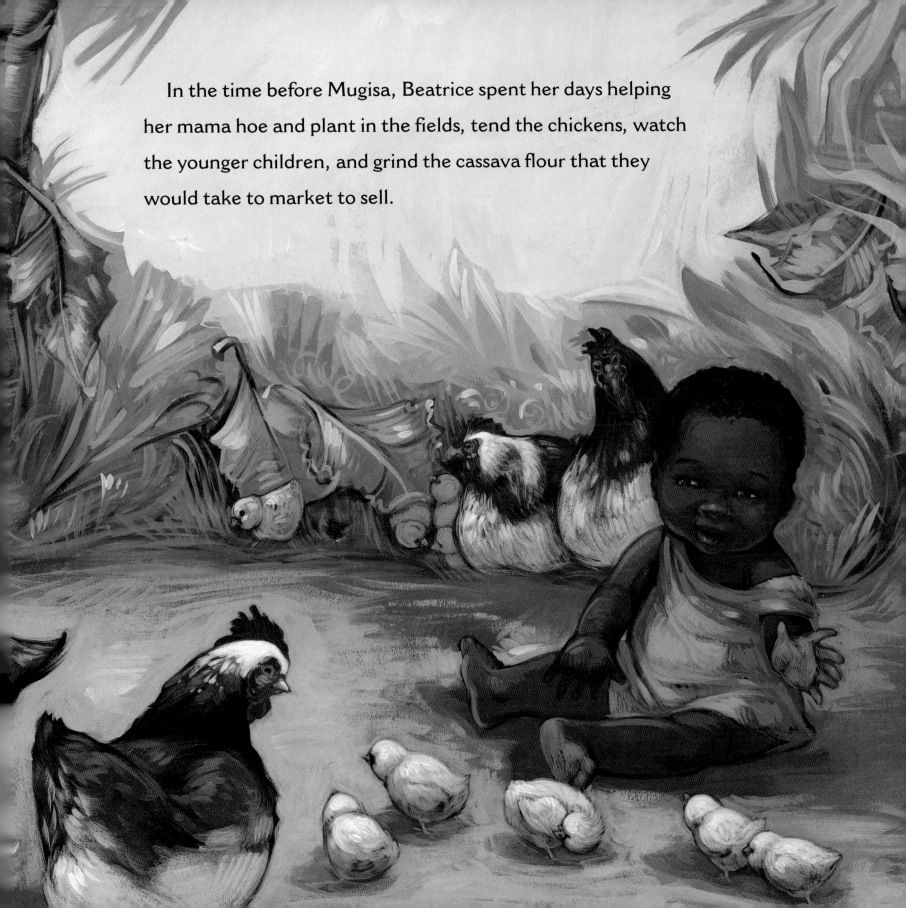

In the time before Mugisa, Beatrice spent her days helping her mama hoe and plant in the fields, tend the chickens, watch the younger children, and grind the cassava flour that they would take to market to sell.

Once in a while, when she was tending baby Paskavia, Beatrice would stop by the schoolhouse. Often, the students had carried their long wooden benches outside to work under the cool shade of the jackfruit trees. Then Beatrice would stand quietly off to one side, pretending she was a student, too.

Oh, how she longed to be a schoolgirl! How she yearned to sit on one of the benches and figure sums on a small slate chalkboard. How she wished to turn the pages of a worn copybook and study each word over and over until it stuck in her mind like a burr.

"I'll never be able to go to school," she would sigh. "How could I ever save enough money to pay for books or a uniform?"

One day while Beatrice was busy pulling weeds, Mama came to her with dancing eyes. "Beatrice, some kindhearted people from far away have given us a lucky gift. We are one of twelve village families to receive a goat."

Beatrice was puzzled. A goat? What kind of gift was a goat? It couldn't get up each morning and start their charcoal fire for cooking. It couldn't hike down to the stream each week and scrub their dirty clothes clean. It couldn't keep an eye on Grace, Moses, Harriet, Joash, and Paskavia.

Her long fingers tugged patiently at the weeds. "That's very nice, Mama," she said politely.

Then Mama added, "It will be your job to take care of our goat. If you do, it can bring wonderful things."

Beatrice looked up at her mother. "Will this goat come soon?" she asked. "Because I would like to meet such a goat."

Mama laughed. "Good things take time. First I must plant pastures and build our goat a shed."

Beatrice nodded slowly. Surely Mama knew what she was doing. "I will help you," she declared.

For the next few months, Beatrice worked harder than ever. She helped Mama collect the posts for the shed walls, then lashed the posts together with banana fibers. She planted narrow bands of stiff elephant grass along the edges of their cassava field. She put in pigeon trees and lab lab vines between the banana trees.

Finally, one day Beatrice's goat arrived, fat and sleek as a ripe mango. Beatrice stood shyly with her brothers and sisters, then stepped forward and circled the goat once. She knelt close, inspecting its round belly, and ran her hand along its smooth back. "Mama says you are our lucky gift," she whispered. "So that is what I will name you. *Mugisa* . . . luck."

Two weeks later, Mugisa gave birth. It was Beatrice who discovered first one

kid and then, to her surprise, another. "Twins!" she exclaimed, stooping down to examine them. "See that, my Mugisa? You have already brought us *two* wonderful things." Beatrice named the first kid *Mulindwa*, which means expected, and the second *Kihembo*, or surprise.

Each day Beatrice made sure Mugisa got extra elephant grass and water to help her produce lots of milk, even though it meant another long trip down to the stream and back.

When the kids no longer needed it, Beatrice took her own first taste of Mugisa's milk. "Mmm. Sweet," she said, mixing the rest into her cup of breakfast porridge. Beatrice knew Mugisa's milk would keep them all much healthier.

Now, each morning after breakfast, Beatrice would head off to the shed to sell whatever milk was left over. "Open for business," she would say, in case anyone was listening.

Often she would spy her friend Bunane coming through the banana groves.

"Good morning, Beatrice, Mugisa, Expected, and Surprise," Bunane would always say. Then he would hand Beatrice a tall pail that she would fill to the top with Mugisa's milk.

When Beatrice finished pouring, Bunane would hand her a shiny coin, and Beatrice would carefully tuck the money into the small woven purse at her side.

Day after day, week after week, Beatrice watched the purse get fuller. Soon there would be enough money for a new shirt for Moses and a warm blanket for the bed she shared with Grace.

One day, Beatrice returned from collecting water and noticed Mama frowning and counting the money in her woven purse. Beatrice put down the water can and rushed to her mother's side. "Mama! What is it?" she asked. "What's wrong?"

As she looked
up, Mama's frown
turned to a small
smile. "I think," she
said, "you may just
have saved enough to
pay for school."

"School?" Beatrice gasped
in disbelief. "But what about all the other things we need?"

"First things first," Mama said.

Beatrice threw her arms around her mother's neck. "Oh, Mama, thank
you." Then she ran to where her goat stood chewing her cud and hugged
her tight. "Oh, Mugisa!" she whispered. "Today *I* am the lucky one. You
have given me the gift I wanted most."

The very next week Beatrice started school. On the first morning that she was to attend, she sat proudly waiting for milk customers in her new yellow blouse and blue jumper, Mugisa by her side.

Beatrice felt nervous and excited at the same time. Mugisa pressed close, letting her coarse coat brush softly against Beatrice's cheek. "Oh, Mugisa," Beatrice cried. "I'll miss you today!"

Then she thought again about all the good things Mugisa was bringing. Mama said that soon Surprise would be sold for a lot of money. "It will be enough to tear down this old house," she had explained. "We will be able to put up a new one with a steel roof that won't leak during the rains."

Beatrice heard a rustle and noticed Bunane heading toward her with his empty milk pail. He eyed her new uniform and sighed. "You're so lucky. I wish *I* could go to school."

Beatrice reached out and touched Bunane's arm. "I've heard that your family is next in line to receive a goat."

A smile crossed Bunane's face. "Really?"

"Really."

Then Beatrice kissed Mugisa on the soft part of her nose, close to where her chin hairs curled just so, and started off to school.

Afterword by Hillary Rodham Clinton

Several years ago, Heifer International—an organization I have known and admired for a long time—invited Page McBrier and Lori Lohstoeter to East Africa to research a children's picture book. *Beatrice's Goat*, a true story about a nine-year-old Ugandan girl, is the result of that trip. It is a heartwarming reminder that families, wherever they live, can change their lives for the better. To do it, they need three things: resources, training, and community support.

Through Heifer, Beatrice's family received all three. They received a goat that provided nutrition and income, knowledge of how to care for this precious gift without harming the environment, and a supportive community that looks forward to sharing the benefits as Mugisa's offspring multiply and are given to an ever-widening circle of families. Now that Beatrice and her brothers and sisters have milk to drink, they are no longer malnourished. The steady income from the sale of the extra milk has allowed Beatrice to attend school for the first time, as well as assuring her family that there will always be money to buy badly needed medicine, clothing, and supplies. Soon, another family—and another, and another—will enjoy these same benefits.

In my travels across this country and around the world, I have seen that there are still too many children who lack the opportunity to grow up with good health, a quality education, and a hopeful future. The story of Beatrice is an invitation to all of us to support those efforts that provide resources, educate families, and lift community spirits.